MY EASY-TO-READ STORIES

Illustrated by Ken Morton
Stories by June Woodman

ISBN 0 86112 631 9
© BRIMAX BOOKS LTD 1990. All rights reserved.
Printed in Portugal for Chad Valley Books.
242-246 Marylebone Road, London. NW1 6JL.
Printed in Portugal by EDIÇÕES ASA - Divisão Gráfica

Contents

8

The Forgetful Spider

Spider is putting on his shoes.
He is going to Kangaroo's
party. He counts his shoes
as he puts them on.
"One, two, three, four, five,
six, seven . . ." Only seven
shoes for EIGHT feet!
"Oh dear, I have lost one
of my shoes," says Spider.
He looks in his house but he
cannot find the shoe anywhere.

He goes to look for the shoe.
He meets Elephant. Elephant
is busy picking oranges.
"Hello, Elephant. Have you seen
my shoe?" asks Spider.
"No," says Elephant, "and I am
far too busy to look for it.
If you see Alligator, tell
him I will bring oranges
to Kangaroo's party."
"I shall probably forget,"
says Spider.

15

Spider sets off to look for
Alligator. As he runs along,
one shiny shoe falls off.
Spider does not see it.
Alligator is on the muddy
river bank.
"Hello, Spider," shouts
Alligator. He waves his tail.
SPLOSH! The mud splashes
spider's shiny shoes.

Spider forgets all about
the oranges.
"Look at my shoes!" he cries.
"They are not shiny now."
"Sorry, Spider," says Alligator.
Spider counts his shoes.
"One, two, three, four,
five, six . . ."
"You have lost two shoes,"
says Alligator.
"Have you seen them?"
asks Spider.
"No," says Alligator.

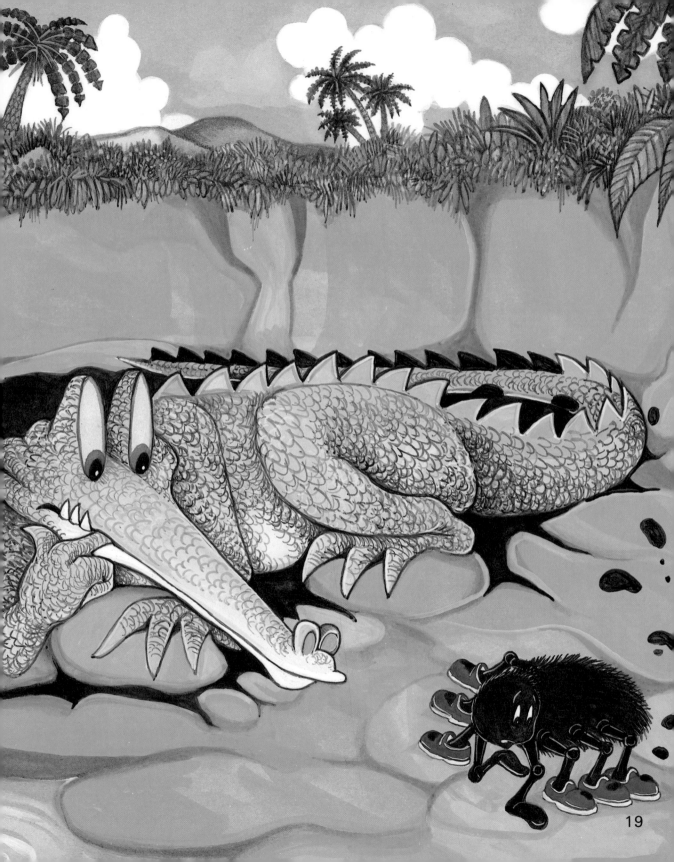

"Go and ask Mouse," says
Alligator, "and tell her
I will bring a cake
to Kangaroo's party."
"I shall probably forget,"
says Spider. He sets off
to look for Mouse. As he
runs along, another shoe
falls off. But Spider
does not see it.

Boom! Boom! Boom!
It is Mouse. She is playing
her drum. What a noise!
"Hey Spider!" says Mouse.
"Where are your shoes?"
Spider forgets all about the
cake. He counts his shoes again.
"One, two, three, four, five."
Only five shoes for eight feet.

23

"I have lost three shoes now,"
says Spider. "Do you know
where they are?"
"No," says Mouse. "Have you
asked Lion? Maybe he can
help. If you see Lion, tell him
I will take my drum
to Kangaroo's party."
"I shall probably forget,"
says Spider.

Spider sets off again.
As he runs, another shoe
falls off. He does not see it.
There is Lion. He is asleep,
as usual, under a tree.
Lion opens one eye.
"Hello, Spider. You have lost
four of your shoes," he says.

Spider forgets about the drum.
"Oh, not another shoe," cries
Spider. He counts his shoes.
"One, two, three, four . . ."
Four shoes for EIGHT feet.
Lion is much too tired
to help Spider look for them.
"Ask Kangaroo," says Lion
with a yawn. "She may know."

"Oh, Spider," says Lion,
"tell Kangaroo I will bring
flowers to her party."
"I shall probably forget,"
says Spider. As he runs off,
another shoe falls off.
But still he does not see!
He meets Kangaroo.
"Hello, Spider. Where are
your shoes?" she cries.

Spider forgets about the flowers.
He counts his shoes.
"One, two, three . . ."
Only three shoes left.
Spider begins to cry
"Cheer up, Spider," says
Kangaroo. "You are just in time
for my party."
"Party?" sobs Spider. "Oh dear,
I forgot about your party."

Look. Here comes Elephant.
He is carrying some oranges
and one of Spider's shoes.
Along comes Alligator with
a cake and another shoe.
There is Mouse carrying her drum
and another shoe. Lion has
some flowers and another shoe.
Spider begins to count.
"I have three shoes. That makes
four . . . five . . . six . . . seven."

Poor Spider. Still only
seven shoes for eight feet.
But Kangaroo says, "Hey Spider.
Look in my pouch."
There is the lost shoe.
"Remember! You gave it to me
yesterday to clean it,"
says Kangaroo. "Bring me
the other seven tomorrow
and I will clean them too."
"Thank you," says Spider,
"but I shall probably forget."

Here are some words in the story.

counts	muddy
lost	another
busy	asleep
party	opens
forget	tired
shiny	yawn
falls	pouch

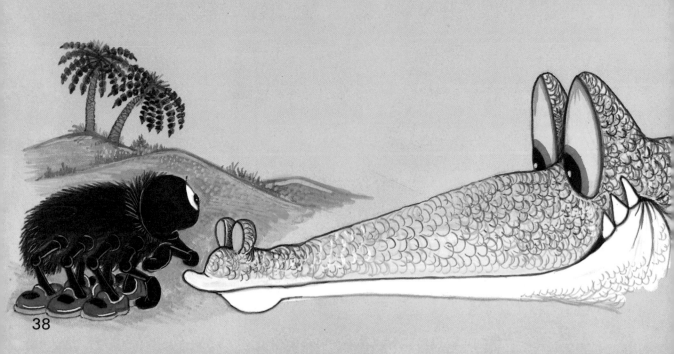

Here are some pictures in the story.

shoes

oranges

cake

drum

flowers

39

40

The Clumsy Alligator

Alligator has big feet. He has a big tail too. Sometimes he trips over his big feet. Sometimes he trips over his big tail. And sometimes he trips over everything. Then all his friends laugh. They call him the clumsy alligator.

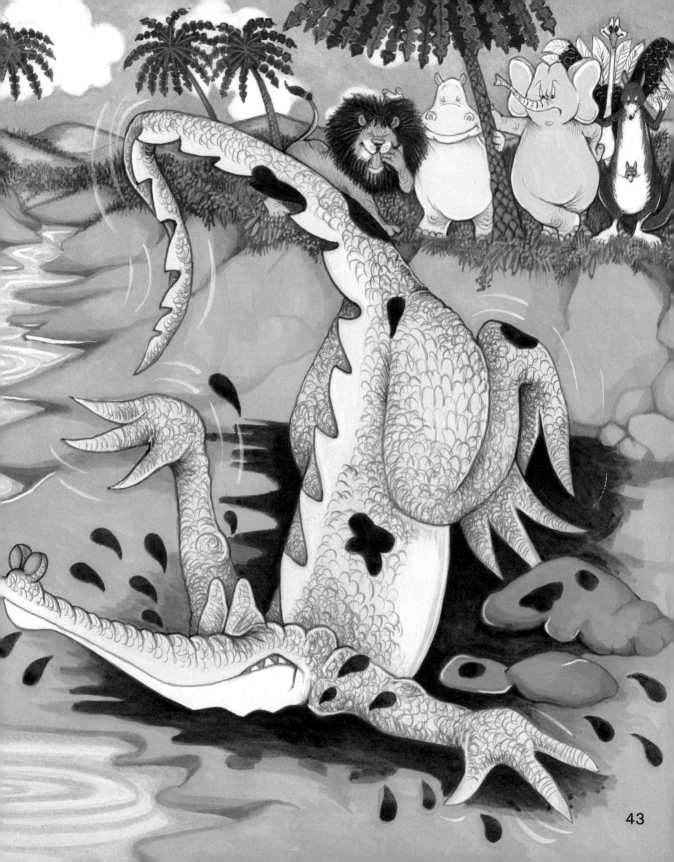

43

One day Alligator is walking
along when he sees Ostrich
picking plums.
"Hello, Ostrich," he shouts.
But Alligator does not see
the log Ostrich is standing on.
He bumps into it. CRASH!
Ostrich tumbles to the ground.
The bucket lands on her head.
"Oops," says Alligator.

Alligator helps take the bucket off Ostrich's head.
"Stay away from me, Alligator," she cries. She gets up and runs off over the stepping stones to the other side of the river.
"Sorry, Ostrich," shouts Alligator.

47

He turns away and goes to look
for his friend Lion. He sees
him lying in the grass. Lion is
asleep as usual. Alligator
runs up to his friend.
But he does not see his tail.
He steps on it very hard.
"Aaaarr," roars Lion.

49

"Oops!" says Alligator.
Lion is very cross.
"You clumsy animal," says Lion.
"I am going over the river
to find a quiet place to rest."
Lion goes across the stepping
stones.
"Sorry, Lion," says Alligator.
"Stay away from me," roars Lion.

Alligator heads back to his muddy bank. His friend Spider comes to see him.

"Hey Alligator," calls Spider. "Look at my new shoes!"

Alligator waves his long tail. Bits of mud go flying through the air.

53

Spider starts to run but it is
too late. SPLASH!
Down comes the mud, all over
Spider's new shoes.
"Oops," says Alligator.
"Look at my new shoes,"
moans Spider.
He runs away from Alligator.
He goes across the river on the
stepping stones.

"Sorry, Spider," shouts Alligator.
"Stay away from me," cries
Spider. Alligator decides to go
and see his friend Kangaroo.
She is picking flowers with
her baby and Hippo.
"Hello," calls Alligator.
He runs up to them.
He does not see the flowers
by the path.

57

"Watch out," cries Hippo
but it is too late. Alligator
crushes all the flowers.
"Oops," says Alligator.
Baby Kangaroo starts to cry.
Kangaroo picks him up and
puts him into her pouch.
"Come on, Hippo," says
Kangaroo. "We shall go
over the river."
They cross the river on the
stepping stones.

59

"Sorry, everyone," shouts
Alligator.
"Stay away from us," calls
Hippo.
Poor Alligator! He sits down
beside the crushed flowers.
He feels sad.
"Nobody likes me because
I spoil everything," he says.
"I wish my feet and tail were
not so big and clumsy."

The sun goes in and it gets very cold. The wind begins to blow and the raindrops start to fall.
It rains and it rains.
Soon the river is full.
Alligator can hardly see the stepping stones at all.

He sees his friends on the
other side. He runs down
to the river.
"Help! We cannot get back!"
they all cry.
"I can help," says Alligator.
He steps into the river. He digs
two big feet into one bank,
and two big feet into the other.
"Jump on," he calls.

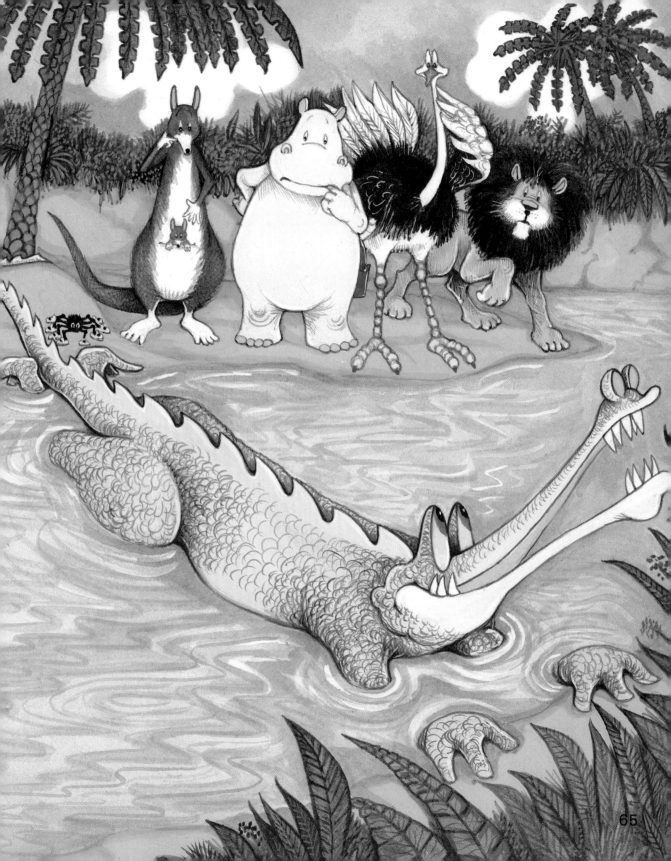

One by one, the animals step onto Alligator's tail and walk across his back to the other side of the river.

"Three cheers for Alligator," says Kangaroo when all the animals are safely across.

"We are very pleased to have a friend with such big feet and such a big tail."

Alligator smiles a very big smile.

Here are some words in the story.

trips	mud
clumsy	flowers
picking	crushes
plums	digs
tail	bank
quiet	jump
waves	smile

Here are some pictures in the story.

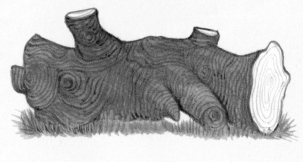

log

bucket

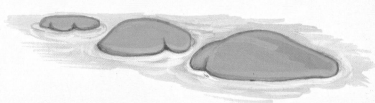

stepping stones

raindrops

river

The Lazy Lion

It is the Jungle Sports Day.
The sun is hot and the path
is dusty. Lion is looking for
somewhere cool to rest.
"I need a good, long sleep,"
he says.
Soon he comes to the river
and stops for a drink.
Alligator is up a tree.
He is tying flags onto
a long string.

"Hey Lion! Can you help me?"
calls Alligator. Lion yawns.
"Not today. I am much too
tired," he says. "But why
are you tying flags, Alligator?"
he asks.
"Because . . . wo–o–o–o . . ."
Alligator trips over the
flags. SPLAT. He lands
in the mud.
"Never mind," says Lion, and
he goes on down the path.

He sees Kangaroo come bouncing
by with her baby in her pouch.
"Hello, Lion," shouts Kangaroo.
"Are you ready for the big day?"
"Not today, Kangaroo,"
says Lion. "I am much too
tired. What big day?" he asks.
"Sorry, Lion," says Kangaroo.
"Must be going. In training,"
and away she bounces.
"Never mind," says Lion.

Lion wanders on down the dusty path. Elephant is under the trees blowing up balloons.

"All these balloons," he says grumpily. "Will you hold some for me, Lion?"

"Not today," says Lion. "I am much too tired." Lion begins to walk away. He does not see the balloons lift Elephant off the ground.

Lion looks back. "Why are you blowing up balloons, Elephant?" he asks. But Elephant is not there. He is floating away above Lion's head.
"Never mind," says Lion.
He turns and walks on in search of a quiet place to sleep.

81

Lion sees Spider trying to put
on his running shoes.
"Can you help me tie my shoes?"
asks Spider. "I forget how
to do it."
"Not today, Spider," says Lion.
"I am much too tired. But why
are you wearing running shoes?"
"I forget," says Spider, "but I
know there is a good reason."
"Never mind," says Lion, as he
walks on.

Parrot is trying to wind up
his stopwatch.
"Hello, Lion. Hello, Lion,"
says Parrot. "Can you help?
Can you help?"
"Not today. I am much
too tired," says Lion. "But
why are you winding up
a stopwatch?"
"Today is the day, today is
the day . . ." Parrot begins.
"Oh never mind," says Lion.

"That Parrot always says everything twice," says Lion as he gets back to his den. Ostrich is waiting for him. She has Lion's invitation to the sports day. "Hello, Lion," whispers Ostrich, starting to blush. She holds out the invitation.

"Not today, Ostrich," says Lion, "I am much too tired. What is it about, anyway?"

But Ostrich is so shy she puts
her bucket over her head
and she runs away.
"Never mind," says Lion.
He is too lazy to look at
the invitation.
"I think I will get a drink
before I settle down," he says
to himself. He wanders slowly
down to the river. Lion has
a drink and falls asleep.

He does not see that he is
lying on the starting line.
He does not notice the other
animals lining up for the first
race. He does not see Kangaroo
bouncing up and down. Or Spider
with his running shoes on. Or
Hippo on tip-toes. Or Alligator
tripping over his feet and
falling into Ostrich.

He does not see Mouse standing on a box, holding a starting pistol. Or Parrot holding the stopwatch.
Mouse calls out, "Ready, Get Set . . ."
BANG! She fires the starting pistol. Lion wakes up with a start. He jumps to his feet and runs off as fast as he can.

Lion runs past all the other animals. He runs through the finishing tape and keeps going until . . .BUMP! He crashes into Elephant. Elephant has just landed with his balloons. "Out of my way, Elephant!" shouts Lion. "Someone is shooting at me."

95

All the other animals come
running up to Lion.
"Well done, Lion," they all
shout. "You have won the race."
"In a world record. In a world
record," says Parrot.
"Have a balloon," says Elephant.
"Not today, Elephant," replies
Lion. "I am far too tired.
I must find somewhere
for a quiet sleep."

Here are some words in the story.

dusty

stops

tying

training

bounces

wanders

quiet

wearing

twice

waiting

blush

lazy

starting

past

Here are some pictures in the story.

flags

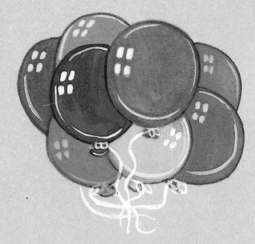

balloons

running shoes

stopwatch

invitation

The Shy Ostrich

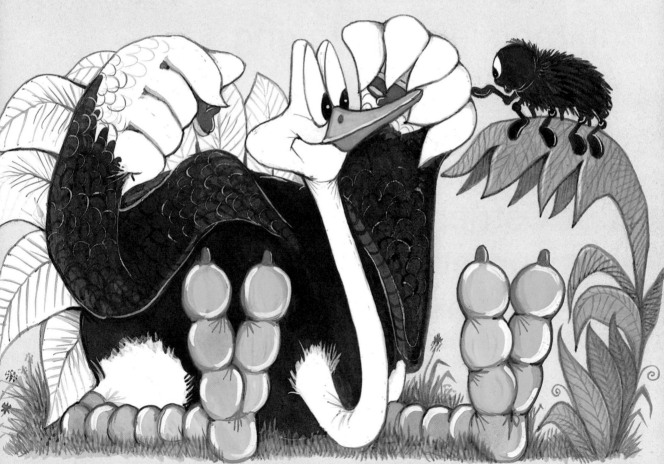

The animals are playing bat
and ball. The bat is a branch.
The ball is a coconut.
Elephant likes to bat. All the
animals enjoy playing.
All except Ostrich.
"Come on, Ostrich! Join in the
game," calls Kangaroo.
But Ostrich goes red and puts
her bucket over her head.
She is too shy to join in.

Ostrich wanders off by
herself. Soon she bumps into
the trees in Elephant's orange
grove. She hears a noise and
takes the bucket off her head.
She sees Monkey taking
Elephant's oranges. Ostrich
wants to stop him but she is
too shy.
"What shall I do?" she
whispers to herself. Then she
thinks of something.

Ostrich puts her head in the bucket and makes a loud noise. "Oooeraaah!" she booms. It sounds just like Elephant. "Elephant is coming!" cries Monkey. He drops the oranges and scampers off. Ostrich picks up the oranges. "Put them down!" says a big voice. Elephant has come back. "Why are you taking my oranges?" he shouts crossly.

107

Ostrich tries to explain.
"I . . . I . . . Oh dear."
She is too shy. She puts her
bucket over her head
and runs off.
Elephant picks up his oranges.
"Stupid bird," he says.
Ostrich keeps running until
she reaches Spider's house.
She hears Monkey again.
He is filling Spider's shoes
with stones.

109

"What shall I do?" whispers
Ostrich to herself.
Then she thinks of something.
She finds a stick and picks up
her bucket. She taps on her
bucket with the stick. Faster
and faster she taps. It sounds
like Spider.
"Spider is coming," yells
Monkey. He drops the shoes
and runs away.

111

Ostrich starts to empty
Spider's shoes. Just then
Spider appears.
"Hey Ostrich. What are you
doing with my shoes?" he asks.
Poor Ostrich tries to explain.
"I . . . I . . . Oh dear." She is too
shy. She puts her bucket over
her head and runs away.
"Funny bird," says Spider.

Ostrich slows down as she reaches Kangaroo's home. She takes the bucket off. She sees Monkey again. He is messing up Baby Kangaroo's toys.
"What shall I do?" whispers Ostrich. Then she thinks of something.

115

She picks a berry and she draws two eyes and a nose on her bucket. She puts vines on top for the hair. She finds a chalky stone and draws a big, scary mouth. She puts the bucket on her head and stands up in the long grass.

"Whoo! Whoo! WHOOO!"
shouts Ostrich.
Monkey looks up.
He sees a scary face
in the long grass.
"HELP, A MONSTER!"
he screams. He drops the toys
and runs for his life.
Ostrich takes off her bucket
and begins to pick up all the
toys. Then she hears a noise.

119

Someone is coming along the path. It is Kangaroo.

"Oh, Ostrich," she says. "What are you doing with Baby's toys?"

"I . . . I . . . Oh dear." Ostrich is too shy to explain. She hides in her bucket and runs off. Kangaroo picks up the toys. "Strange bird," she says.

121

Ostrich sits down and she
begins to cry into her bucket.
"I . . . I . . . I never took
Elephant's oranges. I never
put stones in Spider's shoes.
I never played with Baby
Kangaroo's toys."
"I know, I know," says
a voice. It is Parrot.
"I saw it all. I saw it all.
It was Monkey. It was Monkey."
Parrot likes to say things twice.

123

"I told everyone. I told
everyone," says Parrot.
Here they all come now. Monkey
is with them. He looks very sad.
"He tried to tickle Lion while
he was asleep," explains Mouse.
"If you promise to be a
good Monkey, we will let
you go," says Kangaroo.
"I promise," says Monkey and
he runs away.

"We must have a party for
Ostrich," says Kangaroo.
"She is such a clever bird."
So they have a party. They all
sing and dance. Everyone joins
in the fun. All except Ostrich.
She sits in a corner with
her head in her bucket.
She is so shy.

Here are some words in the story.

join	booms
game	scampers
grove	stick
hears	yells
noise	scary
taking	monster
whispers	clever

Here are some pictures in the story.

branch

coconut

stones

vines

toys

129

The Noisy Mouse

Mouse is very little.
She has a little nose,
two bright little eyes
and four little pink feet.
But she has a VERY BIG VOICE!
When she sings and bangs
her drum she makes
a VERY LOUD NOISE!

133

One day Mouse makes up a new song. "Boom, Boom, Boom," goes her drum. "I can play on the big bass drum," she sings very loudly. "Yes," says Mouse, to herself. "That's just right for the Parade." She wants to try the song on her friends.

She marches off to find them.
Ostrich is picking flowers.
"Listen to this, Ostrich!"
shouts Mouse. She begins to
bang on her drum and she sings,
"I can play on the big bass . . ."
"Ooooh!" moans Ostrich.
"You make my ears ache!"
She hides her head in her
bucket and runs away.

Mouse goes marching on.
Lion is sleeping in his den.
He is wearing a flower necklace.
"Listen to this, Lion!" shouts
Mouse. She begins to sing.
"I can play on the big . . ."
Lion jumps up, banging his
head on the roof.
"Aaaarrr," roars Lion. "You
make my head ache!" He puts
his paws over his ears.

139

Mouse marches to Hippo's pool.
She sees Hippo and Alligator.
"Listen to this, you two!" shouts
Mouse. "I can play on the . . ."
Alligator jumps up with a start.
He sinks his teeth into Hippo.
"Eeeeeee," cries Alligator.
"You make my teeth ache!"
"Aieeeee," cries Hippo. "You
make my . . ." Mouse runs off
before Hippo can finish.

141

Mouse goes marching on.
Giraffe is picking flowers
from the top of the vines.
"Listen to this, Giraffe!"
shouts Mouse. "I can play on . . ."
Giraffe looks down at her.
"Oh! You make my neck ache,
Mouse," says Giraffe.

143

Mouse goes marching on.
Kangaroo is washing Baby.
"Listen to this, Kangaroo,"
shouts Mouse. "I can play . . ."
Kangaroo gives a jump and
drops Baby. He falls
in the water – SPLASH!

145

"Ow," cries Baby Kangaroo.
"You make my tail ache."
"You are too noisy, Mouse,"
says Kangaroo. "Try to play
quietly. Put this sponge on
your drumsticks. And sing
in a whisper."
"I'll try!" shouts Mouse.

"The Parade is starting!
The Parade is starting!"
squawks Parrot. Elephant
is in charge.
"Get into line!" he says.
The animals all line up.
There are flowers everywhere
for the great Flower Parade.

149

"Lead on, Mouse!" orders
Elephant. The Parade sets off
with Mouse at the front.
She begins to play the drum.
"Tap, tap, tap," goes the drum
very quietly. Mouse whispers,
"I can play on the big bass drum."
"What did you say, Mouse?"
asks Giraffe.

151

Spider misses a beat and bumps into Ostrich. She drops her bucket. Alligator trips over it. Monkey steps on Lion's tail and Lion grabs at Kangaroo. Baby falls out of her pouch and everyone ends up in a heap. What a mess!

153

"Oh dear! Oh dear!" cries Parrot.
"We can't hear the beat!"
complains Hippo.
"We can't keep in step!"
cries Spider.
"It's all my fault," says Kangaroo.
"Make as much noise as you
can, Mouse."
"Yippeeeee!" cries Mouse.

So they all line up again.
"Boom, Boom, Boom,"
goes the drum.
Noisy Mouse starts to sing,
"I can play on the big bass drum.
And this is the music to it.
Boom, Boom, BOOM!
goes the big bass drum.
THAT'S the way to do it!"
What a great Flower Parade!
WHAT a noisy Mouse!

Here are some words in the story.

bright   ache

voice   washing

noise   whisper

bass   charge

parade   everywhere

marches   heap

moans   line

Here are some pictures in the story.

drum

necklace

pool

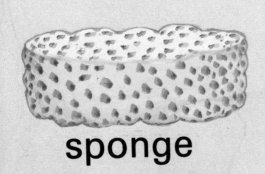

sponge

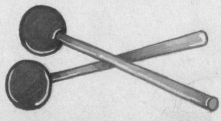

drumsticks

The Grumpy Elephant

Elephant sits down under
one of his orange trees.
Then he gets up again.
"What a bumpy place,"
he grumbles.
He tries another place.
But he gets up again fast!
"Ow!" he yells.
He turns around to look at
the place, but he cannot see
a bump anywhere.

Spider comes rushing up.
"Elephant, Elephant!" he calls.
"What?" grumbles Elephant.
". . . I forget," says Spider,
"but it is very important!"
"You are a very forgetful
Spider," says Elephant.
He goes off to look for
a softer place to sit.

Soon Elephant meets Ostrich
and Hippo. They are putting
straw in a bucket.
Suddenly, Monkey rushes up
and runs off with the bucket.
Hippo runs after him.
"What are they doing?"
asks Elephant crossly.

Ostrich is very shy.
She turns bright red.
"The straw is to make bricks,"
she whispers. "We are going
to build a . . ."
"Speak up, you shy Ostrich.
I can never hear what
you are saying,"
says Elephant.
But Ostrich is too shy.
She runs away after Hippo.

Elephant goes down to
the river.
Alligator is scooping up
big piles of mud.
"What are you doing?"
asks the puzzled Elephant.
"Getting mud for . . .oops!"
He trips over his big feet
and lands on his face
in the mud.
"You clumsy Alligator!"
says Elephant.

171

Elephant is still looking for
a soft place to sit down.
"Boom! Boom! BOOM!"
Here comes Mouse with
her drum.
"Will you help me make
some ropes?" she asks.
"What do you want
ropes for?" asks Elephant.
But Mouse makes so much
noise on her drum,
he cannot hear what she says.

"You noisy Mouse!"
grumbles Elephant. "I cannot
hear you." Elephant walks
away and he finds Lion
lying outside his den
in the sunshine.
"What are they all doing?"
Elephant asks Lion.
"Don't ask me," yawns Lion.
"I know. You were asleep
as usual," sighs Elephant.
"You are a very lazy Lion."
"At least I am not grumpy,"
says Lion.

175

"I am not grumpy," grumbles
Elephant as he wanders
away down the path. Soon he
comes to Kangaroo's place.
She and Baby are dragging
logs along the ground.
"What are you doing?"
asks the very puzzled Elephant.

"You're late!" says Kangaroo. "Hurry up and carry these logs." Elephant is still puzzled but he does as he is told. He picks up the logs and follows Kangaroo and Baby.

They reach the place where
the others are working. Ostrich
and Hippo are building a wall.
Alligator is digging a hole.
Mouse is tying ropes.
Kangaroo shows Elephant how
to put the logs in the ground.

Soon everyone has finished.
Elephant stands back to look.
"What is all this work for?"
he says grumpily.
Then he understands.
"It's a fort!" he says
in surprise, "and a castle
and a cave."
"It's our adventure park,"
says Kangaroo.

183

Spider runs up, very excited. "I remember now, Elephant," he says. "I came to see you but you were asleep. So I put a knot in your tail. It was to remind you to help build the adventure park. But when I came back, I forgot."

"Silly Spider," says Elephant.
"I never forget anything."
Elephant sits down.
"Ouch!" he grumbles,
standing up again fast. He
looks at the knot in his tail.
"You forgot about that,"
says Spider, smiling.

187

Here are some words in the story.

bumpy

build

scooping

important

den

mud

dragging

puzzled

wall

hole

tying

grumpily

excited

remind

Here are some pictures in the story.

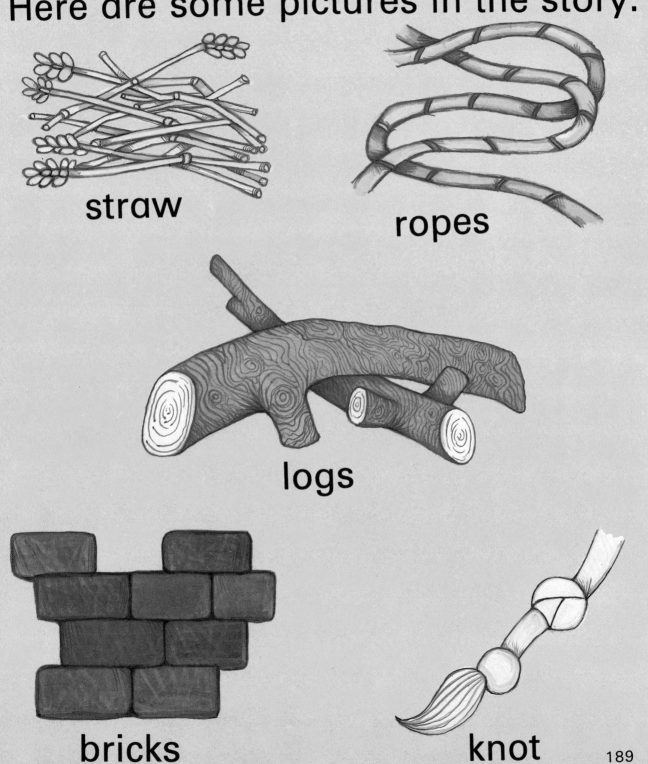

straw

ropes

logs

bricks

knot

189